# Theodore &
# the Enchanted Bookstore

# *The Adventures of Robin Hound*

by

K. Kibbee

Illustrations by J.H. Winter

Theodore and the Enchanted Bookstore: The Adventures of Robin Hound

For more information, to inquire about rights to this or other works, or to purchase copies for special educational, business, or sales promotional uses please write to:

Incorgnito Publishing Press
A division of Market Management Group, LLC
300 E. Bellevue Drive, Suite 208
Pasadena, California 91101

FIRST EDITION

Printed in the United States of America

ISBN:   978-1-944589-44-8

10 9 8 7 6 5 4 3 2 1

*To all the smart little Corgis everywhere.*

# Contents

# Part One

## Sanitarium Sam and the Bewildering Bic

Sam had always been a man of few words . . . not because he struggled with them . . . but because he savored language, and selected each word as carefully as a newborn's name. Yet, as Theodore's voice reverberated through the forest, the typically articulate shopkeeper found himself thoroughly befuddled and utterly speechless.

Following the Corgi's wondrous and shocking feat of speech, several minutes passed with Sam in a slack-jawed stupor and Theodore tilting his head back and forth before a voice disquieted the forest again. This time it was Sam's.

"Did you—? Did you just talk?"

Theodore blinked a few times and shifted his eyes this way and that, almost simpering. "I suppose I did."

"But— What— But you— And we— And where—?"

In a flash, Sam was up and pacing the dusty dirt road onto which they'd materialized, little Pigpen poofs tracking his every step. He needled his temple as he went, staring off into nothing with glazed, vacant eyes. "OK—so we were in the bookstore," he began, "And then there was some kinda hurricane or freak natural disaster. And then, all at once, we were here. Wherever here is."

The shopkeeper's eyes cleared as they fell from the horizon and landed on Theodore, who'd been observing his master's actions from the comfort of a wide tree stump. There was a quaking, uncertain quality to Sam's voice as he recounted, "And then—you could talk."

Theodore bobbed his head in agreement. "Yup. And then I could talk."

Sam shuddered. Then he resumed his stalking and his far-off expression. He'd made it only a couple of strides this time when a noise in the near distance caused him to pause and gaze northward. Theodore replicated the same line of sight and arched a furry brow as clanging and shouting joined the fray of sounds. Then, quite suddenly, the clatter fell off and a motley collection of capped heads began to breach the skyline, just above a slight rise in the hillside to the north. One by one they surfaced, like little mole heads emerging from the ground, until there were nine in total. The heads then fleshed out to reveal full-bodied men beneath them, one quite portly and another as big as a beast, with the remaining seven of average stature. The men approached swiftly and were within shouting distance of Sam and Theodore before Sam had managed to capture even one of his elusive words.

"Aye—who goes there?" called a man from the middle of the group.

Sam became unstuck and ventured towards the rabble. "Hello there! I'm Sam—Sam Moore," he greeted, suddenly grounded by such an easily answerable question.

The man who'd addressed Sam was nearer now—nearer than his compatriots. He wore a fine, bycocket cap of deep velvety green, with a red feather stuck through its side. He was devilishly handsome and grinning as wide as his face would allow. "Well then, Sam Moore," he crooned upon approach. "What brings you to Sherwood Forest on this fine, May day?"

Sam's dumbstruck daze returned in furious fashion as the green-capped man came to a standstill in front of him and was then joined by his menagerie of peculiar cohorts. When the shopkeeper failed to reply, the man glanced at Theodore and, eyes a-twinkle, asked, "What? Dog got your tongue?"

The band of men snickered, particularly the largest one. He kept on long after the others' laughter had died down, snorting like a St. Bernard that Theodore had once seen jogging beside its owner on an especially hot August afternoon. The man in the feathered cap seemed to tire of the bestial noise quickly, and stepped closer to Sam, who was still frozen on the spot.

"You have some unique finery here, friend," the

man observed, narrowing in his sparkling blue eyes on Sam's chest. "Can't recall that I've seen such trinkets fashioned to a garment before. What do you call this?"

Sam peered downward, at his shirt pocket. "This?" he asked, fingering a vinyl sleeve protruding from his flannel. "Oh—this is just a pocket protector. You know—to keep your pens from leaking all over?"

Sam fished a bright red pen from the depths of his pocket and held it out. "See."

The capped man jerked as if he'd just seen Caesar's ghost. He dropped his head, arched his shoulders, and narrowed his eyes to slivers—pinning his full attention to the innocuous red pen. "What kind of witchery is this?" he growled as the men flanking his sides drew hands to an assortment of previously sheathed weapons. Theodore tensed on his stump.

A nervous giggle from Sam echoed through the woods and grew more threadbare as it dissipated. "N—. No witchery here. It's just a pen. A Bic, I think."

The capped man kept a wary distance and gaped at the pen as though it might be quietly hatching a plan to impale him. Meanwhile, one of his men—a dark-haired fellow with a formidably bushy beard—mused, "Perhaps it's a wand, Robin?"

"Aye, a wand!" echoed the pudgiest of the nine men. "And here's the spell book what goes with it!"

Robin spun on his heels to face the round little man, whose muddy eyes and shiny bald head were both glistening in the noonday sun. "What's that, Friar? A spell book, you say?"

"Indeed!"

The Friar waddled towards an open book that lay just a few short feet from Theodore's stump. Its pages were flapping in the gentle breeze but, as the Friar approached and absorbed the wind's gust with his long robe, they fell still. He flipped the book closed, clamped a hand on its spine, and pulled it to his face. His eyes lingered on the cover for a moment or two, and then they began to swell, until Theodore thought they might just pop right out of their sockets. "R-. R-. Robin—," he stammered, drawing back and towards his feather-capped captain.

Robin made a cavalier glance over his shoulder, seemingly unalarmed by the Friar's dramatics. Yet, as his blubbering friend neared and thrust the book in his face, Robin grew suddenly and starkly pale. "What is the meaning of this?" he half-shouted at Sam.

Sam's eyes grew to match the size of the Friar's. His skin blanched as ghostly as Robin's. "Meaning of what?" he echoed in sincere confusion.

Robin, who'd accepted the book, now held it out in front of Sam's face as though it was a dirty diaper, and boomed, "THIS!"

Sam dipped his head, squinted through his slightly askew glasses, and read aloud, "The Tale of Robin Hood."

"Aye! The Tale of Robin Hood! The tale of ME? Of ME! How came you by such a thing?" Robin hammered. "Are you a man of Nottingham's? Are you a man . . . not of God?"

Just behind Robin, the Friar let out a curdled gasp, and . . . if such a thing was possible . . . the fellow grew another shade paler with the same breath. Meanwhile, Robin's lividity had restored his normal hue and infused it with an angry red. His chest ballooned as he bore down on Sam with eyes that could've melted magma.

"It's a book. Just a book," Sam sputtered in reply. "I— Look— I'm as confused as you are here. I mean . . . I don't even know how I got here. C'mon . . . Sherwood Forest—really? And so what—you're Robin Hood, and Friar Tuck? And you there—yeah, you—the big fella," he continued on, pointing at the Yeti of a man who eclipsed his group of friends, "I suppose you're Little John?"

The mammoth man gave Sam a dumb smile and said, "Aye. Have we met?"

"Oh, lordy!" Sam clapped an open palm to his forehead and rolled his eyes, yowling, "I've gotta be dreaming!" His engorged pupils made a second revolution and, as they settled, they became very clear, as did the voice that followed them. "That's it," he decided. "The talking dog, Sherwood Forest—this band of Merry Men. It's all a dream—just one, big ole' crazy bookworm's dream!"

Robin's men looked on silently as the shopkeeper delighted in his revelation. Sam was beaming and bobbing his head feverishly when a sandy-haired gent next to Little John sneered sideways under the cloak of his hand and told the group, "Well, boys, I think we've got ourselves a nutter."

"Heard that," Sam snapped.

"Oh, like you heard the talking dog?" the man goaded him. He glanced briefly at Theodore, took an automatic double-take at the Corgi's wee spectacles, and then shook his head like it was an 8-ball that had just given an impossible answer.

Sam's face screwed up. He shot eyes at Theodore, who'd remained still enough to pass for a taxidermied statue throughout the heated exchange. "Show 'em, Theo," he urged.

Theodore didn't move. His hair didn't even bristle.

"C'mon, Theodore—show 'em! Talk— like you did before."

The Corgi blinked.

"Please?"

Theodore's eyes widened and he shared the brief-est empathetic brow-scrunch with Sam before lapsing into a long, drawn-out yawn.

The men erupted into laughter, which thinly veiled the names—"Crazed loon," "Sanitarium Sam," and "Kook with the book"—that passed between them. They slapped backs and filled the air with their hearty hysterics, every bit the embodiment of their legendary merriment. Robin's eyes were shining with tears when the group finally quieted. He gathered his senses and then looked upon Sam as one might a child who's just said something comically innocent.

"I can't decide if you're a fool or a liar, Sam Moore," Hood told the shopkeeper. "But I make it my business not to trifle with either." He then turned to his men—a few of whom were still choking on residual chuckles—and decided they'd "Best be off, before that nance, Nottingham, could catch wind of a new jester for hire," and ushered them into the marmalade sunset.

Sam and Theodore looked on in shared silence as the men faded gradually into the beyond, but every time their laughter trickled from the horizon, the little Corgi would tense in his spot, and give Sam a guilty glance. Once the troupe had entirely vanished from sight, a small "Sorry" peeped from Theodore's stump.

Sam spun to face his beleaguered companion. "Ah hah! I knew it!" he spat, pointing an extended finger at the dog like a cocked gun. "I knew I heard you talk!"

The shopkeeper paused briefly, bunched his brows together, and weakly added, "Well, either that, or I am completely mad, and you're not talking now, either."

Theodore slunk from the stump, trailing his back end like a massive caterpillar might. "No—I'm talking," he promised, "and I was before, too."

Sam's face screwed up again. "But why—? Why didn't you just then . . . when I asked?"

"Did you see those guys? They were looney tunes!" Theo sputtered. "They'd have probably decided I was magic and tried to squeeze golden eggs out of my rear end!"

Sam stifled a chuckle, but his bewildered expression persisted. He still had brambles and dirt clods peppering his hair from the earlier rough landing on the road, and between the mussed hairdo and crimped smile, he did indeed make for a convincing Sanitarium Sam.

"I dunno how I can talk," Theodore confessed, sensing his friend's confusion. "Well . . . I guess it's more that I don't know why you finally understand me. I was always tryin' to tell you stuff before. It's like you weren't listening—until now."

Sam stared on, still with the look of an escaped mental patient from a Wanted poster. Theodore was near to him now, and the Corgi's voice was soft and comely as the little dog went on, "I told ya' before . . . I think we went inside the book. I dunno how, or why, but once I could see the words . . . read the words . . . it just all came to life."

"Came to life?"

"Yeah. Robin Hood—the story—Sherwood Forest. I could read it all, see it all—through the glasses, and—."

Sam jerked on the spot, like he'd just been goosed. "The glasses—those glasses," he said, pointing at Theodore's cocked head. "Where did you get those glasses anyway?"

Theodore blinked, and his eyes briefly crossed as he examined the frames. "A funny little man gave 'em to me," he told Sam, teetering back and forth on his stubby legs, trying to get a better look at the spectacles saddling his muzzle. "He just showed up, gave 'em to me, and whoosh, he was gone. Like magic."

"Like magic?"

"Yup. Magic."

Sam fell quiet again, clearly noodling. He stroked his chin, as he so often did when in deep thought, and Theodore wondered aloud, "Why do you do that, anyway—rub your chin like that? Are you tryin' to coax the ideas out? Sometimes my old mum would pet me like that, when she was tryin' to get me to come out from under the table, or the chair, or wherever I wasn't supposed to be."

Sam grinned. "Kinda, I guess." His hand stopped rubbing and he examined Theodore, squinting pensively. "Your old family—what were they like?"

Theodore's little head dipped towards the earth and he became very quiet for a spell. Then he looked up and softly said, "Not like you."

"Is that good, or bad?"

"Good," Theodore brightly replied, head ticking upward. "Good—like you."

Sam was immediately beaming, and as his assured expression returned, a bit of the crazy faded away. The transformation was brief, however, for he then resumed an inspection of Theodore's glasses, mumbling about "magic little men," and "snarky ole' Robin Hood."

Meanwhile, Theodore's intent eyes flitted around the forest, and beyond. When they returned to Sam, they found him once again pacing the forest floor.

After several minutes of tracking his master's manic bouncing about the grove, Theo grumbled an interjection. "Okay, so I may just be a dog," he prefaced, "but it seems to me that book got us here. And whether it's bewitched, or magic, or made out of old Penny Saver ads in some crazy little fella's hobbit hole—it's gotta be the thing that gets us out."

Sam had stopped pacing somewhere around "hobbit hole" and urged his companion on with arched eyebrows.

"Well . . . I mean . . . don't-chya think?" Theodore asked with a little waffle to his voice.

Sam's lips worked into a screwy smile. "I 'spose so. If dogs can talk, why can't books transport us to the magical lands written in their pages?"

Theodore nodded, suddenly certain again, and his spectacles bounced lightly on his nose. "Where'd that book get to?" he asked, drawing his eyes downward.

Sam followed suit and the two began combing the ground. Theodore's nose quickly led them to a rectangle-shaped outline in the dirt, where the book had previously been. The Corgi made a brief show of his "snooter-sluething," but then deflated. "It's gone," he whimpered. "Robin Hood and his men—they musta took it."

Sam stared hard at the book's impression, which was sandwiched squarely between Theodore's two front paws. His face drooped as his eyes lingered, but as he returned with, "Well then, we'll just hafta find Robin Hood," an ominous rustle came from the bushes, and quickly quieted him.

A foreign voice with a peculiar drawl creeped from the brush. "Did somebody say Robin Hound?"

# Part Two

## Chicken Feathers

Too dumbfounded, or perhaps too frightened to reply, both Sam and Theodore looked on hesitantly as a pair of golden eyes materialized in the same bush that had just addressed them. Its leaves parted to reveal a bulbous nose and a long, wrinkled muzzle that twitched with every sniff. "Did you say you was lookin' for Robin Hound?" the same thick voice asked.

"Robin Hood, actually," Theodore rather emphatically replied. He blinked behind his spectacles, never faltering from his intense stare as the beast in the bushes emerged fully, to reveal a brutish bloodhound with jowls that hung nearly to his knees.

"That so?" the monstrous hound dog trailed.

"Why you lookin' for my fella?"

"Your fella?"

The dog plodded a half-dozen steps nearer to Theodore and the impact of his massive paws on the ground sent little tremors through the earth between them. "Oh yeah," the dog went on, "me n' Robin Hood is partners. He's my fella. Heck—he's my best friend!" A few more plods towards Theodore, and Sam stepped in between the two dogs, abruptly halting the exchange.

"You stay back now!" the shopkeeper barked.

"What? What are you doing, Sam? This dog knows Robin Hood! He could help us!" Theodore sputtered.

Sam maintained his spot, but his head snapped backward to face Theodore. "Waddaya mean?" he asked. "This dog's comin' at you! He keeps barking! And heck—do you see the size of him? I think he's fixin' to make you into Corgi kibble!"

Theodore bunched his muzzle into a confused

little knot. "Nuh uh!" he defended. "He's tellin' me about how he and Robin Hood are buddies—besties, even. Didn't you hear him? He's not gonna eat me!"

The plucky Corgi gave a little huff and then snaked around Sam's legs—out into the open space at the hound dog's feet.

Sam seemed too stupefied to move.

"So you and Robin—you're friends, huh?" Theodore asked of the lumbering dog, shooting a little glare back at Sam as he did so.

"Thick as thieves!"

"Oh, that's great—absolutely great! Do you think you could help us find him then?"

The bloodhound's saggy face seemed to lift slightly as he attempted a smile, but his weighty wrinkles tugged it back down again, leaving him with an enthused yet confused expression. "Sure I could! Sure as I took a sheep-sized bite outta Nottingham's backside!"

"Excellent!" was Theodore's only reply as he

turned to face Sam. He boasted, "See, told ya'!" and his little chest swelled, so that a curly wisp of hair on his sternum stuck out, revealing a pronounced cowlick that neither Theodore, nor his master, had ever seen before.

"Told me what?" Sam snipped. "He didn't eat ya'—yet—I'll give you that much!"

Theodore only glowered in reply, and an epic dog versus man stare-down ensued—the tension of which could only be broken by the hound dog's ceremonious interjection.

"Why you's talkin' to that man?" the perplexed hound dog inquired. "And why is it that he's seemin' to understand everything what you's sayin'?"

Theodore's left eyebrow jerked up as his right eye narrowed. His soft little mouth opened, but then snapped back shut again. He stood still, between Sam and his befuddled new friend, volleying his head back and forth between the two. Before long, quiet words joined the whoosh of his swiveling head—"He thinks you're barking. You think I'm barking mad," Theodore puzzled aloud, as much to himself as his companions. Whoosh, whoosh, whoosh went the head, and "Yup, yup, yup," went the Corgi. "That's it!" he finally exclaimed. "It's just like it was back at the bookstore, back at the shelter, back at my old mum's—dogs can't understand people, and people can't understand dogs. Only dogs can understand dogs."

Sam's suddenly meek tone sounded almost childlike as he whispered, "But I can understand you?" from his spot behind Theodore. The shopkeeper crouched down and the Corgi swiveled his long body around, so that the two were facing each other. Sam's eyes were sparkling.

"Pretty neat, huh?"

Sam smiled. "Yeah, pretty neat."

"Durn it if that isn't the most curiousest thing I've ever seen," came from the hound's direction, but his words drifted away along with his immense shadow as he retreated to the bushes. He returned just moments later, wearing a bycocket cap identical to the one that Theodore and Sam had seen earlier, on Robin

Hood. The feather was a little off, though—not the brilliant, bright red of the original. This looked more like a chicken feather that had been rubbed in clay so as to make it appear red. It was disheveled, too—perhaps plucked from a chicken who'd experienced a nasty case of mites, or who'd been so troubled by the prospect of becoming Sunday supper that he'd worried himself bald. The hound dog seemed proud of his cap nonetheless, and made an awkward bow as he appeared with it on. "You can call me Robin Hound."

Theodore stifled a giggle. He'd never seen a dog wear a hat before. Well, certainly not by choice. "I'm Theodore," he offered, still half-laughing. "And this," he explained, glancing towards Sam, "is my master—Sam."

Sam stepped up beside the Corgi. "Not master," he said softly, smiling down at Theodore. "Friend."

Robin Hound righted himself with a creak, his long lips swaying with the labored motion, and regarded the twosome with warm eyes. "Nice to meet'chya—Theodore and friend, Sam."

\* \* \*

Robin Hound claimed to know Sherwood Forest better than any living creature—man, dog, or otherwise. He "know'd all the hidey places, the scary spaces, and everything in between," and boasted that he could guide them through "super-secret shortcuts" which would lead directly to Robin Hood's camp—on the far northern border of the forest. He advised against the well-travelled paths, "fur the sake o' safety," and, with his plum-sized snooter, sniffed out an overgrown patch of woods that looked to have been plucked straight out of a horror film, before urging them towards it. "'Dis it, 'dis the one," he decided, beaconing them into the shadows.

Theodore wondered if the heavy wrinkles bunched around the hound dog's eyes were obscuring his vision more than he let on. "You sure?" the little Corgi asked. "This looks a little . . . err . . . rough."

Sam was holding up the rear of their caravan and muttered, "Rough doesn't even cover it," under his breath.

"Nope—nose is never wrong. 'Dis it. 'Dis the one that takes us to Robin Hood," the hound decided. He then lumbered into the brushy undergrowth, mowing it down with his wide chest as he went. Theodore trailed behind, thankful for the flattened pathway, but he'd still managed to gather a nice collection of brambles in his fur after only a few minutes.

"Never realized what a good mop you make," Sam chuckled in the background. Theodore forced a growl in response, but Sam pointed out that it sounded "like the mew of a miffed kitten," and laughed a little louder.

They made slow progress with Robin Hound at the head, and as the dog continued on, struggling with the heavy swaths of brush that impeded them, Theo wondered aloud, "If you and Robin Hood are such chummy friends, don't you come this way pretty often? Why's it so overgrown?"

"Err—" and "Ummm—" came along with a fluttering of the hound's velveteen cheeks, but after he explained that he didn't "come 'round this way most

a' da' time," they returned to flouncing up and down with the dog's long strides.

Theodore only nodded his head at Robin Hound's ample backside and tootled along, but soon found himself translating the dog's response to appease Sam's curiosity. The shopkeeper seemed less contented by the explanation and expressed a mounting unease as his eyes darted around the heavy forest, which appeared to be swallowing the three of them in darkness. "I don't know," Sam piped up, his voice a-quiver. "It's getting dark, and I sure don't see any signs of camps, or trails, or—anything."

Robin Hound froze in an instant, and Theodore nearly planted his pointy nose in the dog's derriere. "What's the man sayin'?" he asked.

"Sam, Robin wants to know what you mean."

Sam too had stopped and was glancing around at the ominous stands of trees and clumps of tangled bushes that the receding sun had bathed in blackness. Sam explained, "I just . . . I mean, I keep hearing things. And it sure isn't a camp of Merry Men," he stammered. "Could be all kinds of creepy crawlies out there."

The hound remained still, but his massive, droopy eyes had begun to scan the shadows. "Creepy what'sa's?"

"Crawlies," Theodore echoed. "You know, critters and what-not."

"Critters?" the hound blubbered. He jerked and Theodore noticed that the hairs between his shoulder blades had pricked up. "Like what kinds a' critters?"

"I dunno. Why's it matter?" Theodore replied. He ticked his head to the side and upward, until he could get a better view around Robin Hound's ample derriere. He was nearly certain that a few of the hound's wrinkles were trembling, so he continued on, "I've caught a few varmints in my day, and surely you've wrestled with plenty in these woods!"

"B—. Bu—. But not in the d-da— Dark," came out like the sputter of a cold engine, and was followed by a wail so gut-rattling that it could've come from a banshee. The hound dog leapt into the twilight sky in that same moment, and despite his girth, managed to catch air.

Sam startled in response and came a few inches off of the ground himself, before touching down with a girlish shriek. "What was that?"

Theodore was about to ask Robin Hound the very same question, but the dog had already lit off into the brush. A curdled "Touched me! Sunthin' touched me!" ushered off his loping strides as he faded into the inky pitch of the nearest tree line, and then vanished.

It wasn't long after the hound's cries had died away that the sounds of the forest filled in to replace them—little scratches, and gnaws, and . . . was that . . . breathing? Theodore backed towards Sam as the menacing chatter grew louder. His rear scuffed Sam's shoe, and the shopkeeper bent down, scooped the Corgi up, and drew him in close.

"What was that? What was he baying about?"

"Said somethin' touched him," Theodore offered, his bespectacled eyes fixated on the trees that had gobbled up his new friend.

Sam gulped and squeezed Theodore a little tighter. Meanwhile, the forest chatter had intensified to become almost deafening. Theodore could feel it weaseling into this brain and nesting there. It was a maddening sort of noise—all the clawing, and hissing, and gnawing—combined into one spooky chorus. It grew louder and nearer with each passing second, until the bushes all around them seemed to be teeming with the vibration of ill-tempered creatures. Growls and grumbles called from the shadows, like the whole forest had come to life and planned to devour this man and the little dog who had dared to trespass upon it.

And that's when it happened. Theodore decided. He decided he was powerful. He decided he'd do anything to protect his friend. He decided to fight. He leapt from Sam's arms and into the darkness, baring his bright, white teeth so daringly that they lit the night.

# Part Three

## Roars & Grumbles, Sniffs & Snuffles

Theodore's spectacles helped him to see things he'd never seen, and do things he'd only ever dreamed of doing, but in the thick soup of blackness that enveloped him as he dove into the brush, they showed him only unending darkness. Still, the brave little dog kept his lips curled and his growl fierce, despite the beasties he imagined might be closing in around him.. The ominous sounds that had boomed from the bushes moments before seemed to die to a soft rumble as Theodore cast his gleaming teeth about the void— roars and grumbles ebbing to sniffs and snuffles.

A quick little motion tugged at the corner of Theodore's right eye and the fearsome Corgi followed it just in time to find a toaster-sized hare darting from one patch of undergrowth to another. The animal caught Theodore with its enlarged, frightened eyes, and then scampered away as quickly as it had come.

"Theodore! Theodore! Are you okay in there?" Sam bellowed from the pathway.

"I'm fine," Theodore answered back, watching as two rotund hedgehogs ambled out of the bush into which the hare had just darted. The small creatures also glanced at him, with wide, frightened eyes, and then hurried—much as meatballs with legs could—into the shadows. Theodore sniggered and then backed from the underbrush like an overlong RV, beeping, "Nothin' in here but lil' critters," as he went. Before he'd extricated himself entirely, another disturbance in the foliage announced the return of Robin Hound, who was wearing a crown of shame made of broken twigs and leaves. The hound's head was hung low and, judging by the balm of mud that coated the right side of his droopy face, he'd taken a tumble or two in his hurried retreat.

"I 'pologize," he brooded upon approach. "I got a lil' carried away with myself there."

Theodore studied the hound with kind eyes. "It's

alright," he soothed. "I know what it feels like—being scared."

"I weren't scared!" Robin Hound spat back, straightening himself. "Were that thing that attacked me! Powerful nasty lil' buggar. Only thing to do was ru—."

The hound stopped short, as if he was chewing the words up before they had a chance to escape his mouth. He grew quiet for a moment, took on a thoughtful expression that resembled constipation, and then picked up where he'd left off. "Only thing to do was scare it off. Ya' know—so as it didn't get the two of you."

Theodore looked sideways through his spectacles and choked down a chuckle, but said nothing. Sam seized upon the momentary quiet to ask, "What's he on about?"

"He . . . err . . . ummm . . . he's explaining how he scared away whatever was attacking us before."

Robin Hood straightened another degree. "Darn toot'in I did."

"Oh," came from Sam with an uncertain tone and a stroke of his chin. He eyed the hound dog as he did would-be shoplifters in his bookstore, but shrugged after the brief examination. "Well, that's good," he decided. He then drew his attention back to Theodore. The shopkeeper's eyes were big now, and shone like lit lighthouses behind the glass of his bifocals as he crooned, "You sure were brave back there, Theo. Didn't know German Shepherds came in miniature." He then added a wink that made Theodore's tiny heart swell in his chest.

Theodore was so contented, in fact, that when they bedded down in a motley, makeshift campsite under an old oak and a blanket of stars, he slept soundly all through the night. On occasion, the little Corgi found himself awakened by a whimper or a spooked gasp from the hound dog, but he was quick to return to his own dreams. The following morning, Sam speculated that Theodore "must'a been dreamin' of running a marathon or auditioning for Dancing with the Dog Stars," in his sleep, because he'd spent pre-dawn "kickin' up a storm with those lil' legs."

Theodore wrinkled his nose at this remark and glared at Sam through his upturned spectacles, with an expression that was equal parts snide and studious. He felt momentarily superior until a long, low growl billowed from his stomach and set everyone to laughing.

"Sounds like you need some breakfast!" Sam observed with a chuckle.

"I can rustle us up some grub," Robin Hound offered, mid-stretch. The gawky bloodhound's rear end was pointed at the heavens while his front half skimmed the ground, causing the better part of his wrinkles to slide to his face and bunch into folds that engulfed his eyes. He gave a long, slow wag of his tail along with the offer, batting nearby bushes with it until their leaves fell to the ground like confetti.

Theodore narrowed his eyes by a few millimeters. "What kinda grub?"

The hound dog straightened up and his wrinkles migrated back to their designated areas. His eyes seemed to pop from his head as they reemerged.

"Well, how's you feel about hot cakes, sizzlin' bacon, and spit-fired honey ham?"

The Corgi's mouth instantaneously began to water. Now it was Theodore's eyes that popped.

Robin Hound pulled the wrinkles on his lips up into a tightly drawn bow, and began to laugh a deep, hearty bellow. "Well, friend, we ain't got none o' that! Bah! Where'd you think I was keepin' all that business—in my castle up yonder hill?"

"What's he saying?" Sam needled from the sidelines.

Theodore only grumbled as the hound dog continued on with his simpering, and then he barked, "Nothin'!" back at Sam.

Meanwhile, Robin Hound's merriment had intensified, so that his great, goopy wrinkles flounced up and down with the escalating laughter. He choked on a reply of, "Oh, ain't nothin'," and then turned and sauntered into the tree line, nearly stumbling over his giggles as he went. As his meaty back end squeezed through the trunks of two willow trees, he hollered back, "Foller me!"

Another grumble from Theodore ushered on Robin's shameless exit as he explained, "C'mon, Sam. We're supposed to follow him. Says he'll find us somethin' to eat." And then Theodore copied the galumphing dog's path into the wood. Beyond the willows, the forest thickened and, if not for the wide swath the hound dog had created with his battering ram of a chest, Theodore probably wouldn't have been able to follow him at all. But, as it was, the wee Corgi reasoned that, "Being a big galoot has its advantages," and soon caught up to Robin Hound, who'd paused at a small rise in the landscape that overlooked a shallow valley just below.

"Shhhh—," the hound warned as his two companions approached. "There's a plump lil' rabbit down there, just waitin' to become breakfast."

Theodore crouched into stealth mode—the varmint-catching lineage that flowed through his veins flooding his mind and body with all the moxie and know-how to trap, skin, and probably fine-fillet anything small and furry. Sam copied him, slinking down behind the trunk of a downed tree which lined the ridge. "What are we hunting?" he asked at a whisper.

"Wabbits."

Sam stifled a giggle as Theo hunkered down beside him. Robin Hound's shadow soon eclipsed them both as the dog settled in beside the Corgi, rested his wide head on the tree's trunk, and fixed his eyes on the valley. Only a handful of silent seconds passed before Theodore's hackles began to wilt and he quietly inquired, "Where is it?"

"'Twas right—," was cut short as the hound dog perked at the sight of a brindled brown rabbit, no bigger than an eggplant, that materialized from a bush on the far side of the valley. Theodore became instantly alert—ears a-twitch and pupils swollen. He tensed at the ready, laser-focused on the unsuspecting animal. A great hush fell over the trio as the rabbit ventured nearer to their hiding spot. But then, amid the stoic silence, there was a soft and unmistakable whimper.

Theodore glanced to his left to find Robin Hound

big-eyed and staring at a black beetle ambling along the log behind which they'd perched. The beetle could've been a ball bearing—round and shiny as it was—if not for the formidable pinchers set between its beady eyes. The hound dog glanced nervously in the insect's direction as it drew nearer. Short as its legs were, the little thing was scampering at quite a nice clip, and already nearing Robin's muzzle. The hound's whining seemed to grow louder with each inch of the beetle's progress, and Theodore warned, "Shhh—. You'll spook the rabbit," as quietly as he could manage.

Sam, who'd been tracking the beetle's progress for far longer than either dog realized, sniffed, "It's just a bug," which only seemed to incense Robin Hound.

"B-bu— Bug-g-g," bubbled up like hot popping corn from the hound dog's mouth as the beetle drew dangerously close to him. He shuttered his eyelids and then squeezed them tightly closed, just in time to miss the insect mounting his left jowl. After sensing it there, Robin's eyes sprang back open and crisscrossed to examine the beetle that was now perched at the tip of his wide nose, clapping its pinchers in a menacing display.

Theodore's mandate to "Keep quiet" was eclipsed entirely by a yowl that shook the entire forest as Robin Hound regressed into a series of infantile screeches and then broke into a full sprint. He was quite a sight—the galumphing hound dog—all knees, elbows, and flapping wrinkles. With every clumsy stride, he bayed like he'd been stuck with a hot poker . . . except for on the handful of occasions when he faltered on a rock or a prickly bush, and wailed a little louder. But, to his credit, Robin kept his smart little cap on throughout the entire ordeal.

Meanwhile, Theodore and Sam took to the valley in pursuit of the spooked bunny, and found themselves racing about the forest like twin versions of Elmer Fudd—one with arms outstretched like he meant to catch the wind and the other with a nose twitching so fast that he nearly did.

"You see him?" Sam shouted out after they'd

made a few fruitless sweeps of the underbrush.

Theodore grumbled along with his stomach, and confessed, "Nuthin'!" but continued on sniffing for several minutes before his shoulders hunched in defeat.

"Well," Sam huffed, drawing to a stop. "Don't think I'd-a had the heart to eat him anyway—starving or not."

The Corgi paused, tilted his head thoughtfully, and speculated, "Yeah, me, neither," just as a wail came from over the ridge.

"Got's him—I gots him!" was laced with palpable excitement from Robin Hound as it floated down the hillside and snared Sam and Theodore. The two immediately leapt into action and followed the hound's bays back up the incline and into a small cove, where Robin had cornered the rabbit. The poor creature was panting from fear and exhaustion, and had clutched itself into a tight little ball at the base of a cedar tree, which the hound dog was circling.

"Wow, you actually found it," Theodore gushed

upon approach. He glanced sideways at Sam, and add-ed, "Good thing it wasn't a beetle," which gave them both a little chuckle that the hound pretended not to hear.

"Well then," Robin Hound baited, "I gots him for ya'. You get to it then."

"Get to what?"

Robin sniffed, mid-pace. "Eat'n him up."

Theodore froze and blinked, taken aback. "Sam. He's saying for us to eat it."

"What?" Sam near-burped, glancing nervously at the frightened little rabbit. "Doesn't he know how to—. I mean, shouldn't he—?"

Theodore set eyes on the hound dog, who'd kept his head low enough to count the blades of grass he was still pacing over. "Yeah, Robin—you're the hunt-er . . . the right hand . . . err, paw . . . of Robin Hood . . . shouldn't you . . . ah . . . do the honors?"

The hound stopped pacing. He raised his head, and a droopy eyebrow. "Well, umm—," he faltered, his eyes darting from face to face. "I, um, I . . . I'm not so hungry. Was you . . . you who said you was hungry."

Theodore's eyes narrowed to slivers as he examined the gargantuan dog who seemed to be shrinking before his very spectacles. "Not hungry, eh?" he repeated, making eyes at Robin's Hood's concave belly. "You swallow that beetle or something?"

"Nope," the hound blubbered. "Just not hungry."

"Hey! Look! He's getting away!" Sam interrupted the dogs' exchange as he called out from the foreground—his shrill declaration trailing off along with the bunny as it broke for the brush. A couple of jukes and a jive later—and breakfast was gone.

Robin Hound hadn't shifted an inch to prevent the escape, and Theodore quietly told Sam that the hound's forced apology had had "all the sincerity of a cat renouncing tuna fish" as their heavy footsteps carried them out of the grove.

Silence and grumbling bellies followed the trio as they ventured deeper into the heart of Sherwood Forest, and it wasn't until about an hour into their journey that Theodore finally spoke again.

"Feels like we're going in circles. Feels like we're getting nowhere."

Robin Hound bristled. "Well, that's a bunch a hooey! Only soul what knows these woods better n' me is good ole' Robin Hood, and he'd be trackin' this very same path!"

Theodore, who was fighting a significant build-up of underbrush that had gathered along his low-slung belly, wiggled as he walked, trying to shake it off, while Sam echoed, "Yeah. I know I've seen those three cedar trees before."

There was another dismissive sputter from Robin Hound, who'd kept his nose pointed towards the thick path ahead, presumably to avoid noticing the familiar family of cedars as he passed them. He'd made it only a few steps beyond the towering trio when he stopped dead in his tracks and gulped so low and loud that it rattled their boughs. His long, velvety ears perked just then, and his eyes began darting back and forth across the skyline. "You hear that?" he asked in a near-whis-per.

"Hear what?"

"Dat buzzin'."

Theodore cocked his head, but heard nothing, so he tilted back and raised his opposite leg off of the ground for leverage, so that his satellite dish of an ear was pointed directly at the heavens. "Nope. Nothin'."

Stopped just behind his Corgi companion, Sam puzzled at the two dogs-turned-statues and wondered aloud, "What are we listening for?"

"Dunno," Theodore confessed.

Robin Hound's ears ticked up another notch. He remained very still, but his eyes darted every which-way. "Thought I . . . Thought I heard me a swarm," the dog confessed, easing slightly as he said it.

"A swarm?" Theodore repeated, setting his free foot back on the ground.

Sam perked up in the background. "A swarm? Swarm of what?"

"Ner'mind," was Robin Hound's only reply as he resumed his amble, eyes forward. A moment or two later, his faint yet unmistakable whisper of "Blasted beetles" trickled back to Theodore's ears, and the little dog chuckled lightly. The levity carried Theo for another few miles, but when the same three trees returned like a mocking version of déjà vu, his disposition immediately soured.

"Okay, Robin, now I'm SURE I've seen these trees before!" Theodore announced, glancing at the heavy boughs that seemed to have worked themselves into mocking smiles. "Sam's right—we're going in circles."

Without any bunnies or beetles to take center stage, Robin floundered in the spotlight. "Naw, naw—trees is trees," he blubbered.

Theodore planted his feet firmly in the ground. "NO. These are the SAME trees, and this is the SAME path that we just walked. Are you sure you know where this camp is?"

Now it was Robin who stuck stubbornly in the

ground, Robin who sounded certain. "Course I do! Me n' Robin Hood—we's best pals! He's . . ." the hound trailed off, his eyes growing distant and dreamy. "Well, he's just—he's the best. And he done taught me everything he knows! He knows these woods, and so I knows these woods. And we certainly knows where 'dat camp is."

"I take it from all his caterwauling that he still says he knows how to find the camp?" Sam speculated.

Theodore nodded at his master and then gave the three cedars a root to tip scan. "Nope," he said as his spectacles scooted back to the base of his muzzle, "I just know it. I just know these are the same trees."

Robin Hound let out a snort. "And what does some dull lil' dog with silly glasses know, anyhow? I'm Robin Hound. I know these woods! You don't even belong here!"

Suddenly, Theodore found himself cowering, shrinking into a small ball. He felt flooded with a familiar, sickly sensation that reminded him of his puppyhood, when he'd felt useless, clumsy, and unwanted. He whimpered, "I guess you're right. I don't know," as quietly as a church mouse, and tucked down his nub of a tail, and let himself sink into a shallow little puddle. Sam studied the exchange through anguished eyes, and then approached the beleaguered Corgi.

"Theo—with those spectacles . . . well . . . I bet you can see from here to Narnia. And if you say these are the same trees . . . well then . . . I'd swear they are . . . even if I was a blind man."

Theodore's puddly parts began to firm up. Sam regarded the little dog as if he'd just saved a baby from a burning car, and they firmed up a bit more. Soon, Theo had risen to his feet and was puffing out his chest. "Sam's right," he realized aloud. "I can see really good now, and I'm sure about this. We're going in circles."

Robin Hound guffawed, clearly taken aback. His chest bowed in the same number of inches that Theodore's had just swollen. "W-w-well, waddaya you suggest then?" he spat, squinting through his heavy wrinkles and adding a snarky little "Smarty dog?" before Theodore had a chance to reply.

Theodore didn't reply at first. He took his time, scanning the trees, the forest, his companions—all in a very deliberate and pensive silence. Then his honey-colored eyes began to sparkle as he was flooded with an entirely mad, yet ingenious plan. He looked back at Robin Hound and explained, "We're gonna get ourselves robbed."

# Part Four

## Pop. Pop. Pop. Three jaws dropped

"Sam—do you remember that book you read me a while back—the one about the boy scout?"

Sam nodded.

"Oh, good," Theodore chirped, excitedly pacing the forest floor. "Well, do you remember the part where the boy scout got lost, and so he climbed up to that high ridge, where he could see the main road?"

Another nod.

"Well, that's what we need to do. We need to find ourselves a high spot—a hill, or a big tree or something to climb—something that can help us see out over the forest . . . help us see the road."

Sam's bottom lip jutted out and his brow scrunched into a thoughtful mess of wrinkle lines. He silently nodded again and then immediately began a scan of the surrounding forest. Meanwhile, Robin Hound's own wrinkles deepened as his voice grew shallow. "Road? Why you wanna find the road? Told you—this here path's safer."

"Safer-schmafer," Theodore returned, eyeing the suddenly rubber-legged hound. "We wanna find Robin Hood and, the way I see it, he sticks to the road—where there's people to rob. Ipso-facto, if we wanna find him again, we need to get ourselves out to the road where we found him the first time . . . where him and his cronies are always hangin' out—looking for rich people to steal from."

Robin Hound's great mouth dropped open, but nothing came out. He then proceeded to chew on his lip blubber while glancing nervously about the forest. Theodore waddled over to him, set a small paw on top of his large one, and suggested, "And hey—I bet there's lots less critters and bugs out there . . . on the main road."

The hound yanked his paw back. "I know's that!"

he snapped, adding, "S'not the bugs I'm worried about," in an ominous tone.

"Well, what are you worried about then?" Theodore primly returned.

"Same thing all us rebel types is—that no-good Nottingham. Him and his goons."

Theodore's eyes broadened along with his mind. "Ah, I see," he said, rolling the e's around on his tongue as though trying to hold on to them just a little longer. He briefly panned the immediate area, seemingly in search of some insight that might be hiding in the bushes, and then added, "Well, I'll keep an eye out for him, then!"

Robin Hound grumbled.

"I know you don't think much of 'em, but these spectacles really are . . . well . . . pretty spectacular! I can see great in 'em and I promise—I'll keep a lookout for nasty ole' Nottingham and give you the high sign before he gets anywhere near us."

Robin's eyes reduced themselves to lines on a

crumpled canvas, but when Theodore pledged, "I promise," and gave a confident bob of his head, they unfurled, if only slightly. Unfortunately, when Sam's calls trickled in from the foreground, they shrunk yet again.

"Hey! Here! I think I see it! I think I see the road!" Sam bellowed from a knoll not fifty yards away. He was bouncing and hooting as the two dogs made their way over, and he looked on with bright eyes as they climbed up to join him. "Here, Theo, I'll help you," he offered in greeting, scooping the Corgi up into his arms.

Theodore panned the treetops and then pointed his muzzle in the same direction as Sam's extended fingertip. The road was clear as day. "That's it!" he rejoiced. "You found it!"

Robin groaned, "Yay," with all the enthusiasm of a teenager offered etiquette lessons and forced a glance in the road's direction. "Now what?"

For the slightest moment, Theodore hesitated. Sam, who still cradled the bespectacled dog in his arms, gave the Corgi a little squeeze, which seemed to pop the words right out of him. "We hit that road like it's bricked in gold!"

With a clear path in sight, the threesome made quick work of returning to the main road, although Robin did enough complaining during the short jaunt to make it seem unending. Phrases like "Hope you's all like dungeons" and "They's gonna make us into footstools" were muttered just loudly enough to be heard, yet quietly enough to warrant no reply. By the time the road was in sight, Theodore secretly wished that Robin was a lovely, quiet footstool. Maybe he'd piddle on one of the legs if he were?

"Look! Look! I can already see someone!" Sam exclaimed from the head of their caravan. The salty-haired shopkeeper was motioning frantically towards the road, where two men approached—each atop a chestnut horse with steam rising from its flanks. Both animals were galloping, and the men bouncing in stride. Sam waved at the pair, but by the time he'd managed to clear the brushy undergrowth that ran alongside the road and make himself visible, the men had already passed. It wasn't until some time later that they again heard the clatter of hooves, which was a welcome respite from Robin Hound's incessant mix of complaints and grandstanding.

The hound was mid-way through a seemingly embellished tale of one of his triumphant battles alongside Robin Hood when a familiar clip-clop-clip-clop came ringing down the too-long-deserted road.

"You hear that?" Sam asked, shuttering his eyelids. Robin's long-winded stories, which fell deaf on the shopkeeper's ears, had sent him into what he'd quietly told Theodore was a "yowl-induced stupor," and he'd jerked just before he spoke, as though awakened by an alarm clock.

Theodore, also unwittingly bored into a semi-catatonic state, suddenly perked up and pointed his keen ears towards the horizon. "Horses!" he excitedly answered back.

The tips of the horses' ears appeared first—tiny triangles, flicking this way and that—and then the mop-tops of one, two, three riders all in a row. These horsemen were travelling at a much more leisurely pace than their predecessors, possibly owing to the elaborate headpiece that the middle man wore—which rocked in time with the steps of his steed. This fellow had hair the color of hayseeds, and it curled in tight, little ringlets around his bright eyes. His skin was fair and flawless. He looked sixteen at best. On either side of him rode men with wrinkles and scars, who seemed to carry the weight of many years. Their mounts were accordingly more modest than the one ridden by the chap in the middle—whose horse was dazzlingly white and looked as clean as Sam's ivory Chevy pickup after wash-day. Contrarily, the two muddy bays that flanked either side of him more closely resembled the Chevy after a long day spent driving on wet, windy country road.

"Ooooh," Theodore sounded out, shifting his focus back to the shiny steed and his opulent rider. "That fella there in the middle—he looks just like the kinda guy Robin Hood would rob!"

Sam bobbed his head in agreement. "It's no pocket protector, but that crown looks pretty impressive."

Robin Hound voiced no opinion, but snorted rather loudly and then rolled his eyes at Theodore's hind end as the Corgi toddled into the road. Theo had just cracked open his muzzle to speak when he thought better of it and glanced backward, at his approaching master. "Ho there," Sam awkwardly greeted the men, waving at them. "We . . . err . . . uhh . . . we come in peace."

"They aren't aliens, Sam," Theodore simpered just above a whisper, trying his very best not to grin.

Sam smoothed his rumpled shirt and shook a half-dozen stray twigs and leaves from his mop of hair. He held out his hand just as the men ventured almost near enough to reach it.

"Greetings," the crowned man answered back with a lazy wave of his eyelids. The other two riders said nothing, but sandwiched their horses closer to the fancy fellow as he spoke. All three animals then came to a stop just inches from Sam's quaking loafers, and the crowned man's eyes narrowed. "Be you a peas-ant?"

Sam didn't answer at first, but instead examined the man atop the white horse like he was a particularly difficultJeopardy question. "Huh?"

"A peasant," the man echoed, his youthful fea-tures contorting as he spat. "ARE—YOU—A—PEASANT?"

Sam glanced nervously between the mens' hard-ening faces, then down at himself. He gave his shirt another flat-palmed smoothing out. "Umm, I don't think so," he replied.

The man in the middle screwed his lips into an uncomfortable-looking knot. His once pale cheeks, now flushed red with anger, bunched up to hide the bright eyes that had shone above them only moments before. "You aren't lying, are you?" he seethed, af-fording Sam no opportunity to respond before adding, "because you must certainly know that for a peasant to address royalty would be punishable by death."

Sam gulped. His eyes flitted from the sour man

in the crown to his book-end henchmen, who seemed to be growing darker, nearer, and more beastly by the second. The shopkeeper's spindly legs began to wobble just as Theodore arrived at his heel. Immediately, they steadied.

One of the stoic and previously silent riders sniggered. "What's this? The scabby not-a-peasant-peasant has a ruddly lil' dog what's gonna defend him, has he?"

Theodore silently wished that the rider had remained mute, and then he glanced backward, towards Robin Hound, in search of reinforcements. At first, he found no sign of the formidable dog, but then he spied a bulbous, black nose and two bee-bee-sized eyes peeking out from a large bush at the side of the road. Theodore locked eyes with the camouflaged hound and offered a coaxing nod of encouragement, but Robin Hound didn't budge. The bush began to quiver.

Theodore muttered, "So much for the valiant Robin Hound," before he had a mind to stop himself.

Now the second silent rider jolted on his mount.

"Aye! Who said that?"

Theodore's mouth clapped shut. The sound seemed deafening.

Henchman Number One was still chuckling at his own cleverness, but stopped abruptly at his cohort startled. "What kinda mischief you up to, you not-a-peasant-peasant?"

Sam struggled, and spat, and stammered—but nothing intelligible, or even English, came out. His legs went jiggly again. Theodore stepped around to block them.

"Wasn't him. It was me," the Corgi proudly proclaimed.

Pop. Pop. Pop. Three jaws dropped.

"And he's NOT a peasant."

The men were frozen. Their horses were frozen. Six sets of eyes fixed squarely upon this bold little dog, no bigger than a breadbox, who was speaking just as surely as they had been. Then there was a curdling gasp—a type of gasp that Theodore had heard

only once before, when his young friend Nan had en-
countered a rather sinister and very hairy spider weav-
ing its web over the Fantasy section at the bookstore.
But this time, it came from a man—a man with fair,
curly hair, and the sensibilities to match.

In that instant, the horses spooked, and then they
bolted. Perhaps they would've flattened Sam and Theodore in their departing stampede, had the animals
not been so wary of the diminutive little Corgi, who
was sidestepped like a den of rattlesnakes. When the
dust from twelve heavy hooves settled, Sam and Theo
were thoroughly carpeted in muck, but no worse for
the wear. They were both mid-cough as Robin Hound
emerged from his hidey-bush and sauntered onto the
road.

"Well, then, that was a bit o' luck then, wasn't
it?" Robin jubilantly observed. "Good thing they were
such a mess of cowards!"

Theodore pawed at his spectacles, wiping a fine
fur of dust from their lenses. Once he could see prop-
erly, he gave Robin an exacerbated glare. "Really?

You're callin' them cowards?"

Robin blinked and gazed at the sinking sun, pretending that Theodore's glare didn't carry ten times its heat. "Aye, they was. All that fussin' and wailin' and what-not. Why—they was like a bunch o' little baby childrens, they were."

Theodore snorted.

Sam copied his companion. "He says they're cowards?"

The Corgi arched his eyebrows until they resembled wooly caterpillars inching across his forehead. He nodded.

Sam rolled his eyes.

Robin Hound had begun to spout some nonsense about readying himself for an ambush when a louder, busier, click-clop, click-clop came sounding down the road. The hound dog retreated to his hidey bush faster than a buck on the opening day of hunting season, leaving Sam and Theodore to greet the onslaught of approaching horsemen alone.

"Helloooo!" was a decidedly warmer greeting than the last men had offered them, but when Theodore saw that it had come from the mouth of none other than the emerald-capped Robin Hood himself, the Corgi's stomach sank a little.

"Boss, it's that crazy feller again," followed from the mouth of Little John, whose saucer-like eyes settled on Theodore and began to sparkle like muddy brown water stirred by raindrops. "And he's got his wee talkin' dog, too!"

"Aye, so he does."

Theodore counted up the riders that flanked either side of Robin like bookends and noted that the entire lot of merry men seemed to be present and accounted for. Each of them was simpering, grinning, or seemingly otherwise amused by the peculiar stranger and his curious little dog—save the Friar, who regarded Sam as if the shopkeeper's head might start spinning and dispensing green vomit. Sam, meanwhile, shot eyes towards the bloodhound-shaped bush into which Robin Hound had vanished, silently willing the dog to appear. His voice was but a whisper as he urged, "Psst. Psst—Robin. You're pal's here. C'mon out."

Theodore thought he saw the bush quake, but the hound didn't emerge. Robin Hound's much bolder counterpart, however, addressed Sam without hesitation.

"Well, I expect I can't put much stock in the ravings of a mad man, but as you're the only soul we've seen on the road in hours, I'll ask you, all the same," Robin began as he came to a stop just a few feet from Sam and Theodore. "Have you seen three fellows come by—one a rather . . . kingly . . . sort?"

Sam seemed to shrink in the shadow of Robin's sizeable horse, and his voice was accordingly weak as it peeped out, "Yes."

Instantly, the marauder's eyes lit. "Ah, is that so?"

Robin scanned the tree line and the road beyond, before adding, "And what did this fellow look like—exactly?"

Sam didn't respond as first. He panned the faces

of Robin's men, and just when it seemed he'd mustered up the moxie to speak, one of the men—a portly, red-headed gent—goaded him, "And more importantly, did he have a talkin' horse?"

Laughter exploded like a fire amongst the men, gaining strength as it consumed each and every last one of them. Little John was so tickled that he nearly toppled from his horse, which, based upon its pained expression, would've welcomed the reprieve. Even the Friar momentarily forgot his fears and indulged in the gaiety, wiggling on his mule until it shook like one of those children's rides in front of the Safeway. But Robin was quick to extinguish the blaze and return his attentions to Sam. His air was stoic as he repeated his question a second time: "What did he look like?"

"K-K-Kingly, I 'spose," Sam sputtered. "Yeah, kingly—like you said."

Robin leaned forward on his horse and glared daggers at the shopkeeper, urging a continued response.

Theodore thought he heard Robin Hound rustle in his nearby bush, but the bloodhound never reemerged, and as the silence grew to a lengthy, uncomfortable degree, Sam began raking at his mane of shaggy hair. "I-I-I don't know," he went on. "Kingly—like with a crown, and a white horse, and a snotty 'tude and all. Kingly."

Robin jerked back until he was again upright, and puzzled over Sam for a moment. Then he asked, "With little blonde curls? Like a child's doll?"

Sam nodded. "Yup. That's him!"

Robin beamed. "Splendid!" He flicked at the brim of his bycocket cap, until it exposed a small patch of forehead and a sheen of sweat. "Well then, my man," he said. "Which way did he go?"

"That way," Sam answered back, pointing into the horizon. "Left not a few moments before you arrived."

"Excellent!" was Robin's only reply as he set boot heels to his horse, causing it to rear up and take off at a start. Soon the rest of his men were copying their fearless leader, and racing past Sam and Theodore one blur at a time.

"Sam—the book!" was all Theodore could get out before the tail end of the entourage came to a grinding halt. The Friar, who was little more than a few feet away, spun his mule to face Sam and Theodore. His eyes were engorged. If it was possible, even his mule assumed a flabbergasted look.

"D-di-did you just speak?" the Friar sputtered.

Theodore snapped his muzzle closed. He resisted the urge to shake his head in denial.

The Friar was needling with his eyes, hardening and narrowing them in on the little dog. "You did, didn't you?" he seethed.

Sam interjected with a "Pfft" and stepped up and around Theodore, until only the nub of the Corgi's tail was visible behind his pant leg. "No, of course not. That's . . . well, that's just impossible."

"Impossible! Why, you yourself said he could talk!"

Another "Pfft" came from Sam as he scuffed at the ground with his loafer, stirring up a cloud of dust that hid Theo all the better. "Naw, I was just—. I just—. I think I ate some bad berries in the forest or something."

The Friar glared on as Sam pretended not to notice. A heavy sort of silence grew in the space between them until one of the Merry men—a strapping fellow with a bushy beard—returned to the scene, asking, "Aye-Tuck—what's you on about? We're losin' daylight—losin' the fellas. Robin's gonna be cross if'n we don't catch up."

"Aye, I'm comin'," seemed to be begrudgingly drawn out of the Friar, but as he and the bearded man turned to leave, Theodore materialized from his dust cloud, and recaptured their interest.

"I did talk," was all it took. Both men dropped their jaws and gawked at the little dog who'd just spoken as clearly as they had. Then, they pounced.

# Part Five

## Nasty, Malicious, and possibly Vicious

"Why on earth did you do that?" Sam demanded, regarding Theodore like he'd just lifted his leg on the sofa.

Both the shopkeeper and his canine companion were tethered to the smelly hind ends of horses and dodging the occasional turd that such a position produced as they trailed behind Friar Tuck and his bearded brother-in-arms, who had diverted from the rest of the Merry Men to return their prisoners to camp. After deciding that the talkative little Corgi was "an evil dog," Friar Tuck had made Theo a baby noose and tentatively looped it over the dog's head as if his sinister touch might be contagious. Sam, of course, had been similarly bound and handled with a notable air of caution, after which both men had selected a rope, and with it, a prisoner.

Theodore loped to keep pace with Friar Tuck's exuberant mule, panting. "W-we-we would'a lost 'em if I didn't. We Wou-would—. Would'a lost the book."

The Friar shot eyes over his shoulder and hit upon the chatty little dog. Though Theodore had previously thought it impossible, the man's expression grew even more sour. No wonder his horse was so eager to get home and be rid of him.

"Yeah, but—," Sam countered, raising his shackled hands along with an eyebrow.

"Just trust me," came from Theodore at little more than a whisper, but the Friar glared his way just the same and then barked something about hellfire and brimstone, at which Theodore clapped his trap shut with an audible snap. Nary a word was spoken for the remainder of their journey, which ended at Robin Hood's much anticipated campsite—nowhere near the bumbling hound dog's "shortcut."

Twilight had set in, bathing the camp in weak, warm light. Men milled around the clearing, attending

to tents and campfires, stew pots and hearty laughter. The bearded fellow who'd played captor to Sam for their short journey led both the beleaguered shopkeeper and his little dog to the far end of the camp, where a wooden cage no bigger than a telephone booth sat empty. "In ya' git," he told them, and they obeyed. He'd no more than closed the door when Friar Tuck came skulking by and gave Theodore the stink-eye.

"I think he likes me," Theodore teased Sam.

The bearded man, still securing a rudimentary latch, sniggered. "Friend—either your lil' dog there's real thick in the head, or he's just 'bout crazy as you are."

Sam said nothing, but gave a weak sigh—like something very heavy rested upon his chest. He then dropped his eyes to the hay-lined cage bottom and sunk into its amber waves. Another sigh. A third sigh came as Theodore inched into his master's lap and curled into a ball there, but this final sigh was different; somehow lighter. They sat like that—Theodore fitted perfectly into the arch of Sam's crossed legs;

Sam stroking the Corgi's fine fur—until the sun had vanished and the moon had taken its place. That's when the Friar returned.

"There—there he is!" the Friar roared, gesturing at Theodore with a book that was clamped in his right hand. "Can't you see—? Can't you see how he works his magic, even now—even on the very hand that feeds him!"

A visibly puzzled Robin Hood followed the Friar's emphatic waves towards Sam and Theodore's cage, where the trapped twosome mirrored his confusion. He examined them briefly and then offered, "I've seen many a man take comfort from his dog, Tuck. Don't make it some kinda hell hound, or whatever it is you've branded this creature."

Friar Tuck growled. His face reddened to mimic a beet. "Tis not the beast's beguiling nature that troubles me, Robin—though surely that's of the Devil's doing, as well. Nay, 'tis his forked tongue that vexes me. He spoke, Robin—HE SPOKE!"

Robin Hood did not reply right away. He tipped

up his cap and crossed his arms over his broad chest, studying Theodore all the while. He then told the little dog, "Well then—out with it, beast. Speak if you've the voice to do it!"

Theodore blinked.

"Speak!"

Theodore blinked again. He tilted his head. He gave Robin puzzled puppy eyes.

"SPEAK!"

And so Theodore spoke—offering a very shrill and very dog-like BARK!—following which Robin Hood launched into laughter. "Well, that's quite a frightening little critter you've got there, Tuck," the capped crusader teased. "He's downright nasty and malicious. Possibly vicious! Why—I wouldn't be surprised if he was plotting to steal our souls along with the discarded stew bones at this very moment!"

Friar Tuck let out a low, deep growl which mimicked a cement mixer that Theodore had once heard rumble past the bookstore—and his face turned nearly as ashen as its concrete-splattered belly. "The beast is clearly up to its trickery," the defeated Friar muttered, dropping his eyes. As his focus fell, he fixed on the book in his hand and then raised both his hand and the book into the air with renewed enthusiasm. "But what of this, Robin?" he insisted, shaking it. "What of this otherworldly text—steeped in your secrets and foretelling of your conquests yet to come? Surely this is of the Devil's making."

Robin grinned, and his smile all but glittered. "Ah, nothing more than a child's storybook," he lightly replied. "Some tale pieced together through campfire tellings and whispers passed amongst the peasants."

Robin's grin widened as he fell into silent satisfaction, and Theodore noticed a slight blush warming the woodman's cheeks. The Friar, on the other hand, grew even colder as the color drained from his face.

"I trust this wicked creation about as much as an old hag with a gingerbread house!" the Friar roared, casting the book into the dust beside Theodore and Sam's cage. "'Tis the Devil's work, just the same as these two!"

Robin Hood gave the Friar a soft pat on the back, which seemed to calm the overwound little man. "Awe, Tuck—give it a rest. Come, have some ale. Make merry with me," he pressed, offering another charming smile.

Friar Tuck bobbed his head slowly, as if he'd spent all of his energy, and then followed Robin towards a glowing fire that was surrounded by chattering men—their voices warm and their hands heavy with mugs of drink. A dozen or more fireflies hung over the group—casting a warm, orange light—but as Robin and Tuck joined the circle, the insects scattered and then melted into the night sky like stars. Theodore watched them wistfully for a moment or two before he felt a prod from Sam's index finger.

"Look," the shopkeeper whispered, pointing at the earth near their shared cage. "The book—the one from the store. That's what the Friar was going on about. It's the Robin Hood book!"

Theodore's attention shifted in a millisecond—as if he'd caught a squirrel sneaking through his peripheral vision—and there, in the dirt, just finger lengths away, he saw the very book that he and Sam had been searching for. It was peppered in mud and a bit worse for the wear, but certainly the same book that had transported them to the wilds of Sherwood Forest. Theodore's eyes lit up like the fireflies. "Wowza, it is the book!"

As if on instinct, Theodore dropped to his belly and snaked his paw through the cage bars, swiping at the earth just beyond them. Sam mimicked him from above, but neither could reach the book. Close—but not quite. Somehow, having the book near enough to smell the must on its pages, and yet not being able to retrieve it, seemed worse than not knowing where it was at all. It was suddenly like a bright yellow tennis ball on a high shelf, and poor Theodore huffed and puffed as he continued to strain to reach it.

"It's no good, Theo," Sam finally lamented, pulling his face away from the side of the cage, along with a series of long, thin impressions left by its bars.

"You look a little like a zebra," Theodore chuckled.

"Huh?"

"Oh, the cage . . . from pressing your face—." Theo stopped short as a loud rustle emanated from the brush just a few feet from their ramshackle prison. His ears pricked. "You hear that?"

Sam peered in the direction of the sound, big-eyed. "I did," he whispered back.

The hairs between Theodore's shoulder blades stood on end. His eyes shrunk to razors as he set them on the brush. It rustled a second time, and then trembled in a most unnatural way. Then, a long nose emerged from the waxy leaves, followed by a mess of wrinkles and two twinkling, honey-brown eyes. "Robin Hound!"

The dopey hound dog burst out of the foliage with all the grace of a hippopotamus on roller skates and came bounding towards Sam and Theo's cage. "Hey, fellas!" he excitedly drawled. "Knew I was gettin' close—sure as shootin'! I could smell ya's!"

Sam offered a cautionary "Shhhh" at a low register and glanced towards the campfire, where Robin and his men, now fully soused, were too busy singing and clanking mugs of ale to notice the bumbling dog's entrance.

Robin Hound deflated in an instant, like he'd been caught chewing shoes or piddling on the rug. He sunk without sinking, howled without making a peep. Even his wrinkles seemed to somehow grow longer—heavier. He made up the remainder of the distance to the cage at a slow plod. "I's come to rescue ya'," he offered once he was near enough for his whisper to be heard.

"That's awesome!" was Theodore's initial response, but then he muddled on for a second or two before adding, "But, what about you and Robin Hood? You know—your . . . what was it . . . fiercesome friendship? Can't you just ask him to free us?"

Now, Theodore was sure of it—Robin Hound's wrinkles were growing longer—sagging like hot wax. The dog looked positively miserable as he blubbered, "Well, uhh . . . that may have been a bit of a . . . uhh . . . tall tale I told you's. I, uhh—."

"No worries," Theodore brightly cut in, "I kinda figured . . . well . . . anyway—you're here now, and that's what matters."

The wrinkles stopped melting and Robin's head shot up. "Yup, I shore am—and I'm gonna rescue ya's—just like ole' Robin Hood'd rescue his Merry Men. Gonna get you out and get you all tucked up with a nice camp, nice fire, nice rabbit—only the best o' the best!"

"He gonna get us out?" popped out from overhead as Sam studied the bantering twosome and then locked eyes with Theodore. The Corgi nodded, though with notable trepidation, and Sam mirrored his expression.

No sooner had Robin Hound seemingly redeemed himself than he began pawing noisily at Sam and Theodore's enclosure. Noisily enough, in fact, that he drew the attention of one of the revelers from the campfire, whose head ticked ominously in their direction. "Oye—what you on about over there?" the man wailed through a cloud of fireflies.

The bloodhound leapt into the underbrush and was a quivering ball of leaf-covered cowardice before you could say 'Boo.' The man, contrarily, marched towards Sam and Theodore with his inflated chest leading every step. As he neared them, Theodore noted that he was more boy than man, and clearly not dulled by the same spirits that now haunted his older compatriots. "You best keep your yaps shut," the young fellow cautioned, mustering the manliest expression his doughy face could manage. He cocked a chin towards the campfire and told them, "We've been known to roast us some noisy prisoners."

At this point, the man-boy may or may not have smirked. He then paused for reply, but when none was offered, he cast up the forced glower of a child who'd been instructed to show his meanest, gruffest, most intimidating face. Then he stomped back to the welcoming warmth of the men and their bonfire.

Robin Hound peeked from the bushes only a second or two later. "Coast clear?" he asked.

"Yeah, it's clear," Theodore whispered back. "But

be quiet this time!"

"Quiet? I'm always quiet. Why . . . some calls me 'the Stealth of Sherwood.'"

Theodore's eyes nearly rolled right out of their sockets. "Sure they do."

Robin muttered something inaudible yet undoubtedly condescending under his breath and slogged himself over to Sam and Theodore's cage, where he proceeded to examine the lock that imprisoned them. "Ya might'n be nicer to someone who's rescuin' you," he quietly growled whilst nudging the lock with his wide nose, seemingly under the expectation that it would simply fall off.

Sam quirked an eyebrow and crouched down to address Theodore. "He knows he needs a key, right?"

Robin Hound immediately ceased his nosework and raised his eyes to Sam. "You gots a key?" the dog dumbly inquired.

"Well, no—we don't," Theodore answered back as patiently as he could manage. "If we had one, we'd have been outta here ages ago."

Robin Hound returned a slow, deliberate blink, but no reply, and Theodore was first to fill in the silence. "What about that beardy fella, Sam—that fella who locked us in? Didn't he have a key?"

Sam shot eyes towards the campfire, quickly narrowing in on the chap with the fur of hair wrapped around his chin like a wiry winter scarf. "Ya' know—I think maybe he did."

A swift whip of his head and Theodore too had sights on their frizzy-faced jailer. The Corgi squinted through his spectacular spectacles, conducting a thorough head-to-toe appraisal. "On his belt loop?"

"Yes! His belt loop!"

Robin Hound made a feeble attempt to copy his two friends, but succeeded only in synching his eyes so tightly that they shut altogether. "I don't sees it," he confessed.

"Oh, you will," Theodore assured him. "You just need to get close enough."

# Part Six

## Cowardly Dogs & Flying Tree Frogs

It took a mess of reassurance, a little shaming, and even a bit of bribery (who knew bloodhounds fancied pocket protectors?) before Robin Hound finally consented to brave the minefield of Merry Men and retrieve the key to Sam and Theodore's cage. Of course, by this time the men were little more than a snoring pile of lazyouts, but that did little to diminish Robin's fear. Backlit by the breaking sunrise, the hound's knees knocked in time as he made his way across the campsite towards the bearded key-holder, who was three sheets to the wind and lying with his head in Little John's lap. John was snoring louder than the lot of the men combined, and each exhale he gave sent waves through his sleeping companion's chin scruff. Robin Hound paused as John's snores became impossibly louder, and shot a trepidatious glance back at Theodore.

"S'okay," Theo quietly urged," motioning for the cowardly hound to continue.

Robin's head swiveled back towards the camp-fire, but not before he gave Theodore a look like he'd been asked to dive head first into an open grave. He then arched to tiptoes (which Sam quietly decided was "a most unsettling sight"), and made up the last few feet between himself and the slumbering key keeper. Once he was within swiping distance, he hunkered down low, as though he was about to be swatted with a rolled-up newspaper, and eased his nose towards a shiny rung of keys hanging from the bearded man's belt. Even from the cage, Theodore could see that the bloodhound's entire body had begun to tremble.

Sam squatted down so that he was eye-level with Theodore. Both captives pressed their faces eagerly against the cage bars. "Yeesh—plug a quarter in him and he could pass for one of those vibrating massage chairs down at the mall," the shopkeeper quietly teased.

Theodore stifled a chuckle and asked, "Think he'll get it?"

Sam gulped. "Hard to say."

Oblivious to their banter, Robin Hound was singularly fixated on the keyring that was jangling enticingly with every heaving snore that shook Little John's lap. He moved his snout a millimeter closer; another millimeter, half a millimeter. He could nearly touch it. Only a hair's breadth separated Robin from his prize—until trouble arrived on the wings of a walnut-sized beetle as black as the Devil's heart and twice as nasty. It swooped from the sky, all but dive-bombing the bug-a-phobic bloodhound and sending him into a frenzy of howls. In an instant, the Merry Men jolted awake, and in their semi-inebriated stupor, began fumbling madly for their weapons. Flummoxed and tipsy as they were, Robin Hound was able to make it clear across the campsite and deep into the bush before nary an arrow was slung. As he bulleted past Sam and Theodore, he offered only wide, panic-stricken eyes and a strong gust of wind that sent dust rushing into their cage.

"Wh—. What was that?" was shouted in chorus throughout the campsite, but no one man seemed any more equipped to answer than another. Eventually it was the blowhard man-boy who'd chastised Sam and Theodore on the night prior who spoke up.

"I think . . . 'twas a dog. I caught sight of his hind end, I did. Looked like that ole' hound dog."

Robin Hood straightened his slightly askew cap, grimaced, and then spoke in a voice as slow and thick as molasses. "Not him again. Ratty ole' beast—always trailin' after me in that silly ole' cap. I know Nottingham's the one sending him 'round. Havin' a go at me with that get-up. Thinks he's clever, he does."

"He ain't nothin' compared to you, Robin," the boy swooned.

Another of the men glowered through heavy lids and told the young boy, "Aw, quit your gushin', lad. Save it for your ma, and those lovely maidens you're always on about," which sent waves of laughter cascading through the camp, and turned the boy deep crimson. Even Sam giggled a little, which elicited a glare from his four-legged companion.

"We're sunk now," Theodore grumbled as Sam's grin wilted. "No help, no key, no book."

The Corgi fixed eyes on the book, which was now splayed open from the gust sent along by Robin Hound's abrupt passing. His eyes lingered there briefly and then brightened to rival Sam's collection of ugly Christmas sweaters.

"That's it! The Robin Hood book! The book can get us out of here—out of the cage, out of Sherwood—out of everything! We didn't even need the key. It was here all the time!"

Sam stared through the cage bars and screwed his face up into a pitiful knot. "But we still can't reach it."

"Maybe we don't need to," Theodore mused, scuttling towards the edge of the cage nearest to the book. He poked his long nose through the bars, in turn cinching his spectacles up tight to the bridge of his nose. "If . . . I . . . could just—," came out one choppy syllable at a time as the determined little dog pressed into the bars and squinted with of all his might.

Sam moved in close, so that Theodore's fine hairs were tickling the edge of his pant leg. He too pressed his face into the cage bars and peered out at the prized book. Just as he began to wonder aloud, "What are you—? Are you trying to—?" Theodore's voice boomed, loud and true as he read . . .

"So passed the gentle springtime away in budding beauty; its silver showers and sunshine, its green meadows and its flowers. So, likewise, passed the summer with its yellow sunlight, its quivering heat and deep, bosky foliage, its long twilights and its mellow nights, through which the frogs croaked and fairy folk were said to be out on the hillsides . . ."

The ground began to tremble, and the cage along with it. The air around them stirred, like a waking beast, and a low, haunting howl filtered in—seemingly from nowhere and everywhere all at once. The book's pages flipped to and fro—clapping against one another as though their words were fighting to escape. Theodore hooted, "It's working!" and Sam had no sooner joined him in rejoicing than the Merry Men took note

of the small hurricane mounting on the fringes of their campsite, and rose to investigate. A half-dozen of them approached as the breeze began to pitch and swirl with sticks and leaves and one particularly skinny tree frog.

"It's the end of days!" the Friar wailed, clapping a hand over his heart. He'd no more finished his dooms-day proclamation than the old fool turned white as a ghost and then fainted right there on the spot. A couple of the men came to his aid, while the others slowed to a cautious crawl.

Meanwhile, the wind had grown vicious, and even the fat tree frogs weren't safe. A wild-eyed toad whipped by Sam and Theodore's cage as the storm rattled their bars and tore the roof clean from their prison. Theodore had no sooner suggested that they escape through the opening when he and Sam were suctioned into the book's great vacuum, hoisted into the sky, and then swallowed into its pages.

* * *

Theodore came to on a polka-dot bean bag that smelled faintly of his pee. He blinked his eyes twice, and panned the familiar bookstore, which was bathed in the warm glow of breaking sunrise. A few open books appeared to flutter their pages in welcome, and Theodore felt certain that one of the stuffed unicorns guarding the Fantasy section bowed its head at him.

"Sam! We made it! We're back!" stuck like bubblegum in Theo's throat as he rolled off the bean bag and lit out in search of his master. He began to canvas the store while attempting a second call out to Sam, but this one just came up as a burp.

Sam, his hair mussed and glasses askew, lay just around the corner on a Persian rug that one of the kids from the reading group had affectionately nicknamed, "The Magic Carpet," following an intensely interactive reading of Aladdin. The shopkeeper stirred at Theodore's approach and his smile spread like sweet strawberry jam. "We made it back!" he rejoiced, sweeping the store with delighted eyes.

Sam echoed a second, even more zestful "We made it back!" and then rose, scooped Theo into his arms, and began twirling around and around until they were both a little ill. He'd no more come to a dizzy stop than a loud clatter erupted from the storeroom.

All eyes shot to the back of the store. Both Sam and Theo froze—although Theo was left swinging like a limp ragdoll in the shopkeeper's arms for a moment or two until gravity was done with him. Then there was stillness. And quiet. Eerie quiet.

A painful minute passed. Then two. Then both Theo and Sam jolted as a thrump and a chigga-chigga trickled from the shadows and a dark figure slithered in, eclipsing the doorway to the storeroom.

A low, uncertain growl trickled from the darkness and the hairs on Theodore's neck went rigid as Robin Hood's imposing frame emerged out of the shadows.

# ABOUT THE AUTHOR

K. (Kristine) Kibbee is a Pacific Northwest writer with an affection for all things literary. Kristine's passion for creative writing began in her early youth and led her to the doors of Washington State University, where she studied in the Professional Writing program. Kristine followed her scholarly pursuit of writing by publishing works in The Vancougar, The Salal

Review Literary Review, Just Frenchies magazine, and S/Tick Literary Review. She is presently a regular columnist for Terrier Group magazine.

Kristine's novella, The Mischievous Misadventures of Dewey the Daring, was her first and only self-published release, and is still currently available on Amazon.com. Her middle-grade fantasy novel, Whole in the Clouds, was released in November 2014 with Zharmae Publishing, with a subsequent, expanded edition published in October of 2017 by Incorgnito Publishing Press. The first installment in her YA fantasy series, Forests of the Fae—Devlin's Door, was released in early 2016 with Incorgnito Publishing Press. Book two in the Forests of the Fae series (The Raven Queen) followed in February of 2017, also with Incorgnito Publishing Press.

Kristine's newest series, Theodore and the Enchanted Bookstore was launched with book one, Tale of the Spectacular Spectacles, under the Corgi Bits imprint of Incorgnito Publishing Press, in October of 2017. Kristine regularly engages on a variety of social media platforms and can be followed:

On Twitter @K_Kibbee

On Facebook @ facebook.com/KKibbeewrites

# Credits

This book is a work of art produced by Incorgnito Publishing
Press; Corgi Bits Imprint

Jennifer Collins
Editor

J. H. Winter
Illustrator

Star Foos
Designer

Janice Bini
Chief Reader

Michael Conant
*Publisher*

Daria Lacy
Graphic Production

December 2017
*Incorgnito Publishing Press*

CPSIA information can be obtained
at www.ICGtesting.com
Printed in the USA
LVHW022048251118
598226LV00002B/2/P

9 781944 589448